Fairy Hill

Ruby and the Magic Garden

by Cari Meister
illustrated by Erika Meza

SCHOLASTIC INC.

For Ruby — seamstress for the dreamer

Library of Congress Cataloging-in-Publication Data
Names: Meister, Cari, author. | Meza, Erika, illustrator.
Title: Ruby and the magic garden / by Cari Meister ; illustrated by Erika Meza.
Description: New York, NY : Scholastic Inc., 2017. | Series: Fairy Hill ; [1] | Summary: Fairy Hill's
magic garden has lost its sparkle, and three young fairies, Ruby, May, and Luna, try everything to
restore its magic—but nothing works until Ruby discovers what is blocking the magic, and earns
her wings. Identifiers: LCCN 2016054940 | ISBN 9781338121803 (pbk.) Subjects: LCSH: Fairies—
Juvenile fiction. | Magic—Juvenile fiction. | CYAC: Fairies—Fiction. | Magic—Fiction. Classification:
LCC PZ7.M515916 Ru 2017 | DDC [E]—dc23 LC record available at https://lccn.loc.gov/2016054940

10 9 8 7 6 5 4 3 2 1   17 18 19 20 21

Printed in U.S.A.   40
First printing 2017

Book design by Steve Ponzo

Fairy Hill is a land of sparkle and fun!

Welcome to *Fairy Hill*

There are fairy homes.
There are fairy shops.

There is even a magic fairy garden!

Ruby, Luna, and May live in Fairy Hill.
They are best friends.

They love to learn magic.

"Oops! I lost my ball," says Luna.

"I need more practice."

Ring-a ling-ling! Ring-a ling-ling!

"The Fairy Queen is here!" says Luna.

"Wow!" says May. "She is *all* sparkle!"

"Look," says Ruby,
"that fairy is getting her big wings!
She must have done something
extra brave, kind, or helpful."

"I wonder what my big wings will look like," says Ruby.

"I hope I earn mine soon," says May.

"Me too!" says Luna.

Ruby, Luna, and May still have small wings.
They cannot fly.
They ride on their fairy flyers to get around.

"Let's go to the garden," says Luna.

"Good idea," says May.

"Race you!" says Ruby.

Ruby rides with Ace.

Ace is fast.

"Whoa!" Ruby laughs. "Look at my beard!"

Soon they are at the magic garden.

But it is all brown.

Something is wrong!

"The garden has lost its sparkle!" says Ruby.

"I will fix it!" says May.
May sprinkles fairy dust.
The garden does not change.

"I will fix it!" says Luna.

Luna plays a magic song.

The garden does not change.

Then they hear a sound.
"It is a baby deer!" says Luna.
"He looks lost," says May.

"Do not worry," Ruby says. "We will help you."

"Magic clover helps lost animals find their way home," says May.
But the clover is all wilted.
It has lost its magic.
"What are we going to do?" asks Luna.

Ruby looks at the dirt.
She looks at the flowers.

She spots something shiny.
It is Luna's lost ball.
It is blocking the magic water!

"I will fix it!" Ruby says.
Ruby waves her wand.
The ball lifts into the air.
The water flows.

The flowers start to sparkle.
"You saved the garden!" says Luna.

Ruby finds the magic clover.
She gives it to the deer.
He licks her face and runs home.

Ring-a ling-ling! Ring-a ling-ling!

"Look!" says May.

"Here comes the Fairy Queen!" says Luna.

"You were kind to the deer, Ruby,"
says the Fairy Queen.
"And you fixed the magic garden.
Today you earn your big wings!"

The Fairy Queen taps her magic wand.
Ruby's wings grow.
They sparkle and shimmer.

"Your wings are perfect!" says Luna.
"They are so shiny!" says May.
The Fairy Queen smiles.

"I can't wait to try my new wings," says Ruby.
"Race you!"